GREEK BEASTS AND HEROES

The Fire Breather

You can read the stories in the
Greek Beasts and Heroes series in any order.

If you'd like to read more about some of the
characters in this book, turn to pages 76-78
to find out which other books to try.

Atticus's journey continues on
from *The Silver Chariot*.

To find out where he goes next,
read *The Flying Horse*.

Turn to page 79 for a complete list
of titles in the series.

GREEK BEASTS AND HEROES

The Fire Breather

LUCY COATS

Illustrated by Anthony Lewis

Orion
Children's Books

Text and illustrations first appeared in
Atticus the Storyteller's 100 Greek Myths
First published in Great Britain in 2002
by Orion Children's Books
This edition published in Great Britain in 2010
by Orion Children's Books
a division of the Orion Publishing Group Ltd
Orion House
5 Upper St Martin's Lane
London WC2H 9EA
An Hachette UK company

1 3 5 7 9 8 6 4 2

A catalogue record for this book is available from the British Library

ISBN 978 1 4440 0070 2

Printed in China

www.orionbooks.co.uk
www.lucycoats.com

For Richard,
because he is The Best Husband
(and the Most Understanding),
with love and thanks.
L. C.

For Louise
A. L.

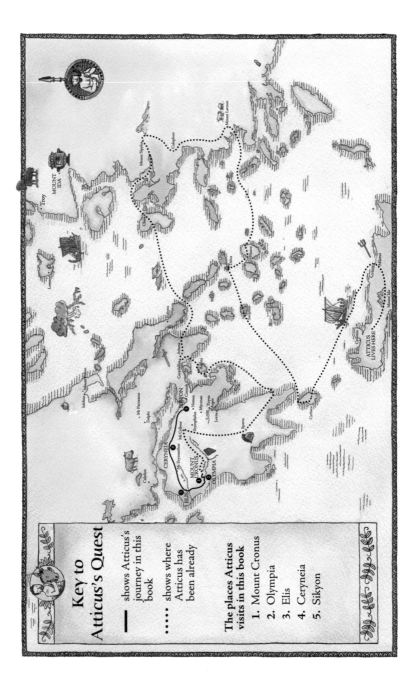

Key to
Atticus's Quest

— shows Atticus's
journey in this
book

···· shows where
Atticus has
been already

The places Atticus
visits in this book:

1. Mount Cronus
2. Olympia
3. Elis
4. Ceryneia
5. Sikyon

Contents

Stories from the Heavens

L ong ago, in ancient Greece, gods and goddesses, heroes and heroines lived together with fearful monsters and every kind of

fabulous beast that ever flew, or walked or swam. But little by little, as people began to build more villages and towns and cities, the gods and monsters disappeared into the secret places of the world and the heavens, so that they could have some peace.

Before they disappeared, the gods and goddesses gave the gift of storytelling to men and women, so that nobody would ever forget them. They ordered that there should be a great storytelling festival once every seven years on the slopes of Mount Ida, near Troy, and that tellers of tales should come from all over Greece and from lands near and far to take part. Every

seven years a beautiful painted vase, filled to the brim with gold, magically appeared as a first prize, and the winner was honoured for the rest of his life by all the people of Greece.

Next day Atticus sat on the very top of
Mount Cronus and watched a snake
sunning itself nearby. He could see the
sea in the far-distant west, sparkling in
the sunshine. An eagle soared overhead.

"You'd better watch out, snake," said
Atticus. "He's looking for supper."

The snake raised its head, and its
tongue flickered, tasting the air.

"I wonder what kind of snakes the
Furies had in their hair," said Atticus
thoughtfully. "Would you like to hear
about them, snake?"

The snake hissed.

The Kindly Ones

When the Titan, Cronus, gave his father Uranus the great wound that sent him running into the outer darkness of heaven, four drops of Uranus's blood fell to earth.

One drop fell into the sea and became the goddess Aphrodite, but the other three drops soaked into the rich soil that lay around Mount Cronus.

Soon three small mounds appeared. The earth boiled and bubbled around them, until, pop, pop, pop, hundreds of snakes' heads came out of each mound.

Finally three fierce-looking women pushed their way out of the heaving soil.

Each had snakes instead of hair, a large
pair of copper-coloured wings, a whip in
the left hand, and a blazing torch in the
right.

"Furies!" they cried harshly as they
emerged. "We are the Furies!"

Then they started
to flap their huge
wings and sniff
about with their
long, pointed noses,
as the snakes on their
heads hissed and
wriggled.

"We will light up the
hiding places of the wicked
ones with our bright
torches. We will whip them to
the ends of the earth and punish them!"
they chanted.

And with a great whoosh of coppery feathers they rose into the air and flew off into the world.

For many years the Furies chased and killed those who were unlucky enough or stupid enough to break their laws, and sometimes they made mistakes.

But eventually Apollo and Athene, who were tired of the bloodshed, persuaded them to put down their torches and whips, and gave them a temple to themselves.

There they became known as the Kindly Ones, and the people were so thankful to be saved from their terrible punishments, that they gave them presents and sacrifices for ever after.

 15

The buildings of Olympia spread out below as Atticus and Melissa came down Mount Cronus. Priests were bustling about under the plane trees as they passed.

"This is where the Festival of Zeus is held," said Atticus. "Every four years, the best athletes in Greece come to compete in the Olympic Games, just over there in the stadium. I expect some of them will be training in Elis when we arrive there tomorrow – the Games are only a few months away."

Atticus stopped under a wild olive tree. "I'll sit and tell you how it all started."

The Games of the Gods

It was a very dangerous thing to be in love with Princess Hippodamia of Elis. Her father, King Oenomaus, had ordered that anyone who wanted to marry her must first race against the team of magic horses which had been given to him by Ares, the cowardly god of war.

If the suitor won, the wedding would take place at once. But if he lost, King Oenomaus would chop his head off.

Pelops (the same one who was put in a stew by his father, Tantalus) had heard of Hippodamia's beauty, and he decided to try his luck. He set off with his own team of magical horses, which had been given to him by the gods to make up for being chopped up and served at a feast by his own father.

"After all my horses came from Zeus himself, so they must be able to beat a team that was given by a coward like

Ares," he said to himself.

As soon as he saw Hippodamia Pelops fell in love with her and she with him.

But Hippodamia didn't know that Pelops had a team of magic horses too. So she bribed a stable boy to loosen a nut on one of her father's chariot wheels, so that it would wobble and go slowly. She wanted Pelops to win.

The stable boy hated King Oenomaus, because his elder brother had been one of Hippodamia's unsuccessful suitors, and had had his head chopped off by the king.

So instead of loosening just one nut, he took them all out, and replaced them with wax ones. "Serve him right if he dies!" he thought with a nasty grin.

The red flag dipped, and the horses raced off. At first they were evenly matched, and the chariots hurtled neck and neck round the course.

But soon Pelops began to draw ahead, and King Oenomaus's chariot began

to wobble as the wax nuts melted. There was an ear-splitting screech of metal as the chariot flew apart, and the king was thrown to the ground.

As Pelops drew up, Hippodamia began to cry and to shake the stable boy, who was standing beside her.

"Wretched wretch! I only asked you to loosen a little nut, so my beloved Pelops would win. Now my father is dead!" she wailed.

The stable boy wriggled out of her grip and ran backwards through the crowd, but Pelops strode forward and seized him. Then he marched him to the nearest cliff and threw him into the sea.

"Before I marry Hippodamia, we shall have a fabulous funeral

 22

feast for her father!" he declared. "We shall invite all the kings and heroes, and afterwards we shall hold games at Olympia, with prizes of gold and jewels for the winners."

The gods themselves looked down on the games and declared them to be such a success that after Pelops and Hippodamia were married they announced that they would hold them every four years.

And so the Olympic Games were created for heroes and heroines from all over Greece to prove their strength and their skill to gods and mortals alike.

Athletes strutted round the streets of Elis,
their oiled bodies gleaming in the evening
sunshine, their trainers scurrying behind
whispering advice.

Although the Games didn't officially
start till the first full moon of autumn,
stallholders were already setting out
souvenirs. Atticus and Melissa strolled
along, enjoying the sights.

"What a pity we can't stay for the Games,"
said Atticus. "Look at that discus thrower!
He must be almost as strong as Heracles!
Poor Heracles, he did have a hard life.
Let's find a shady spot to rest in, and you
can hear how his troubles came about."

The Strongest Man

There was simply no one stronger than Heracles. He was the son of Zeus and the Princess Alcmene, and the great-grandson of Perseus who had killed Medusa the Gorgon.

Even when he was a baby he was so strong that he strangled the two huge spotted snakes the goddess Hera had sent to bite him in his cradle. She hated him because her husband Zeus had run off with his mother.

Heracles' enormous strength meant he was not an easy child to have around a polite palace where people behaved themselves, and didn't run around roaring

and shouting and breaking things. When he was learning the lyre, his huge fingers plucked the strings so hard that they broke. When he sang, his great voice cracked and broke on the high notes.

In fact Heracles hated singing so much that one day he gave his teacher what he thought was a tiny tap with the lyre, and killed him stone dead. After that he was sent away to be a shepherd.

Heracles was much happier in the mountains, where he could wrestle with lions and bears and wolves to his heart's content. Soon stories of his deeds spread all the way to Thebes, where even King Creon heard of them.

"I must have this hero for my son-in-law!" he said, and he summoned Heracles to come and marry his daughter Megara.

Heracles and Megara were happy

 27

together, and soon they had lots of
children. Heracles loved them all and used
to bring them lion cubs to play with.

But one day Hera looked down from
Olympus and saw Heracles laughing.

"I'll teach him to laugh!" she muttered,
and she sent a horrible black cloud of
madness to attack Heracles.

As soon as it touched him, he imagined

 28

he was surrounded by wild beasts, so he killed them all. When the cloud drifted back to Olympus he discovered that Megara and all his children were dead.

"What shall I do?" he wailed, tearing his hair and beating his great chest.

"You must go to Delphi and ask Apollo's oracle for advice," said King Creon, tears running down into his beard.

So Heracles went to Delphi to learn what he must do to make up for the awful crime he had committed.

Now the King of Tiryns at that time was Eurystheus, who was Heracles' cousin. He was jealous of Heracles, because he himself was weak and puny, with arms like sticks, thin yellow legs and a squeaky voice.

When Eurystheus heard that the oracle had ordered Heracles to serve him for ten years, and do ten difficult tasks for him, he was delighted. Hera was pleased too, because Eurystheus was a friend of hers, and she knew she could help him to think up some impossible things for Heracles to do.

So Heracles came to the gates of Tiryns to report to his cousin for orders. For the next ten years he had to do everything that Eurystheus said, but he didn't mind at all. He just hoped that one day he would be able to forget the terrible, terrible thing he had done.

Two days later Atticus was still in Elis. He was sitting on the steps of the Temple of Aphrodite, looking into the sunset, when a travelling player sat down beside him.

The man was dressed in a strange costume, with a moth-eaten lion skin over one shoulder, and he was carrying a mask.

"Coming to see the play tonight?" he asked. "We're acting the labours of Heracles for the Olympic ambassadors – the one about the oxen. It's the first time I've done it, and I'm a bit nervous, to tell you the truth."

"Would you like me to tell you the story to remind you?" asked Atticus.

"My friend," said the actor (whose name was Glaucus), "that would be fabulous!"

Cattle Stealer

King Eurystheus had set Heracles
an impossible task. He rubbed his
hands gleefully as he summoned his
cousin to the throne room.

"I want those nice fat red cows
belonging to Geryon," he squeaked. "And
I want them in a year and a day!"

Heracles sighed. He would have to
hurry. Geryon's island was at the farthest
edge of the Western Ocean, and a year
and a day wasn't nearly long enough to
get there and back.

He ran to the edge of the land and dived into the sea.

Soon he was swimming strongly westwards. But even after he had swum a long, long way, Geryon's island was still not in sight, and Heracles was getting tired. He turned over on his back for a rest, and looked up into the sky. Sailing just above him was Helios the sun god in his golden cloud boat. Heracles swam to the nearest rock and hauled himself out of the water.

Fitting a huge arrow to his bow, he took aim and shouted: "Hey, Helios! Lend me your boat for a bit or I'll shoot you down!"

Helios had no choice, so he steered his boat to the rock, and got out crossly, pulling his chariot and horses behind him.

"I'll need it back," he said sulkily.

"And mind you don't bump it on anything."

Heracles pulled two great craggy boulders off the rock and threw them into the ocean so that he could find his way home. They stuck up above the waves, and sailors in later times called them the Pillars of Heracles.

Then he set the sails, and vanished into the west.

At last he saw a huge island in front of him. It was covered in flat grassy plains, on which several herds of fat, red cattle were grazing.

Heracles landed the boat quietly, and

sneaked ashore. As soon as he had set foot on land, a huge two-headed dog rushed at him barking. Heracles wrestled it to the ground and threw it into a bush.

He set out towards the cattle, but before he could reach them, he was attacked by a hideous giant who was Geryon's shepherd. Heracles punched him in the head and knocked him over. Then he dragged him over to a water-hole and pushed him into it.

Heracles was just rounding up the
last cow when he heard a great roar.

Geryon himself was running out
from his palace. "How dare you steal
my cattle!" he cried, spit and foam flying
from his three mouths.

Heracles calmly fixed three arrows to
his bow, and shot Geryon in each of his
three bodies.

Pluff, pluff, pluff went the
arrows, and Geryon's spindly legs wobbled
as he sank to the ground, quite dead.

The red cattle walked quietly into the boat and Heracles sailed back to the mainland. It took him a long time, as the boat didn't like going the wrong way round the world.

Just as he was giving the boat back to Helios, Hera sent a cloud of her most vicious gadflies to sting the cows, and they scattered everywhere.

Heracles only just had time to round them up on the last day of the year.

He drove them to the gates of Tiryns before dawn the next day and yelled up at the windows.

"Cousin Eurystheus! Here are your cows! I've finished my task!"

Eurystheus looked out smiling unpleasantly. Heracles might think he'd finished, but he and Hera had another couple of things for him to do before he was free.

"Oh Heracles! Come here a minute!" he called.

And poor Heracles trudged into the throne room once again to hear what his next task was to be.

Atticus couldn't believe his luck. After the play was over his new friend Glaucus had invited him to join the travelling players as official storyteller.

First of all they were going to visit some of the places where Heracles had performed his tasks, and then they were walking all the way to Corinth! It was exactly the way Atticus and Melissa had been going themselves.

"It'll be nice to have some company for a change," he said to Melissa. "And we can see all their plays. Tonight after supper they all want to hear the story of the Augean stables. The place they're staying in now is so dirty they can't wait to move out!"

The Dirtiest Job in the World

King Eurystheus of Tiryns had just set his cousin Heracles another terrible task. He had got together with the goddess Hera to think of something really difficult this time, and he rubbed his hands gleefully at the thought of Heracles' face when he had heard what he had to do.

"A little bit of dirt will do him good," he chuckled.

Augeias, King of Elis, had three hundred black bulls and two hundred red, as well as twelve silver and white bulls which were sacred to the gods. He also had herds and herds of wonderful cows. Their mooing kept everyone in Elis awake far into the night, and the clouds of their breath shut out the early morning sun.

Their barnyards and stables were filled with dung to the height of five men, and they hadn't been cleaned out for twenty years. The smell was truly dreadful, and the people of Elis all wore masks over their noses.

Heracles only had a year to clean the stables and barns, and to make the floors spotless enough for King Augeias to eat his dinner off. It certainly was an impossible task.

But Heracles was not going to be beaten by a bit of muck. He sat in the middle of a herd of black and red cows, scratching his head and thinking hard.

Suddenly he heard the sound of rushing water, and then he had an idea. Elis was built between two rivers. If he could only persuade the rivers to flow through the barns and stables, they would be clean in no time at all. And best of all, he could just sit and watch.

Heracles worked hard to persuade the two rivers to move out of their courses, but at last he managed. "It's only for a day," he said

 42

to the river gods, herding the cattle carefully on to a nearby hill.

Next morning King Augeias and the people of Elis saw a wonderful sight. Two great walls of green water were swirling through the mountains of muck, and washing it away to the sea.

Soon the stables and barns were as shining and clean as a spring morning, and that night King Augeias ordered a celebration feast.

"I shall eat it off the stable floor!" he laughed, and he invited Heracles to join him.

When Eurystheus heard of Heracles' success, he flung his crown on the ground and jumped on it. "I'll get him yet!" he vowed crossly as he went to think up another impossible task.

It was days since they had left Elis, and they had walked a long way. Melissa's ears drooped in the heat as she climbed the slopes of Mount Erymanthus, followed by two other donkeys carrying masks and costumes and props.

"Never mind," said Atticus, patting her. "Glaucus says there's a nice cool spring at the top, and you can rest."

After supper, the players lay around the fire, some playing music, others just staring into the embers.

"Come on, Atticus," yawned Glaucus. "Tell us a story to send us to sleep."

"I'll tell you about something that happened just down there by that big cave," said Atticus.

The Biggest Pig

"Come here, Heracles," said King Eurystheus. "I've thought up another task. My people tell me that a huge and horrible boar is roaming through the countryside up by Mount Erymanthus. It's as big as a house, and it has tusks as long as lances and sharper than scissors. It's killing everything it sees, and it seems to be rather fierce. I want you to go and catch it for me. And mind you bring it back alive."

Heracles gathered his weapons and wrapped himself up warmly. It was winter, and snow was falling softly as he slipped out of the palace gates. He was rather looking forward to this task, although he was more used to killing boar than capturing them.

It took him a long time to get to Mount Erymanthus, but at last he arrived, and he walked around the snowy mountain, thinking out his plan.

Suddenly he heard crashing and grunting above him, and the enormous boar appeared out of the bushes, and ran into a large cave.

His little piggy eyes were flashing red
with fury, and his tusks were dripping
with blood and foam. The bristles on his
back stood up like needles, and he was at
least as big as a house, if not bigger.

"Ho! Boar!" shouted Heracles. "Come
and fight me if you dare!"

There was a squeal of rage, and the
boar charged out of the cave again.

But Heracles was too clever for him. He ran off up the mountain like a hare, and the boar galloped behind him. The snow got deeper and deeper, and soon the heavy boar was exhausted. His body sank into the snow and stuck fast in a snowdrift.

Quickly, Heracles bundled him into a strong chain net, and then he carried him on his shoulders all the way to the gates of Tiryns.

"Cousin Eurystheus!" he called. "I've got the boar you wanted!"

But when Eurystheus saw the sharp tusks and heard the great animal squealing and raging to get at him, he ran inside and hid himself in a large bronze jar which he had ordered to be made.

Unfortunately one of his servants had filled it with olive oil. And oh! weren't his best robes sticky and greasy when he finally dared to climb out!

Atticus and the players wandered slowly on through the hilly countryside, stopping to perform in several small villages on the way up to Ceryneia. But soon there were no more houses, and they found themselves on a path through the woods. A herd of deer was grazing in a clearing. One of the hinds looked quite golden in the sunlight, and Atticus pointed at her.

"Heracles caught a deer like that near here," he said.

"Hey!" shouted Glaucus. "Time for a rest and a story! Gather round, everyone!"

The Golden Deer

Artemis had four magical golden hinds which she used to pull her hunting chariot. But their sister was even more beautiful. She had been too fast even for Artemis to catch, and so she lived in the woods, where Artemis declared her sacred and under her protection.

King Eurystheus had heard about the famous hind from Hera, and he knew how much it would annoy Artemis if she were caught.

"If I tell Heracles to bring me the hind," he thought, "he will never dare to offend Artemis, and so he will fail. Then I can punish him."

He summoned Heracles at once.
"Go to Ceryneia, and bring me Artemis'
golden deer," he said. "She will be a nice
ornament for the palace gardens."

Heracles went straight to Ceryneia and hid by a pool in the woods. Sure enough the golden deer stepped out of the trees in the evening light and started to drink. Her coat was like sunshine, and her horns shone like fire.

As Heracles started to chase after her, her hooves flashed bronze lightning, and she ran faster than the wind.

Heracles chased the golden deer for a whole year from Istria to the land of Tauris, but eventually she sank down, exhausted, and Heracles tied her feet together and carried her back to his cousin in Tiryns.

"How pretty she is," said King Eurystheus as he stroked her soft ears and released her among his flowerbeds.

The golden hind only stayed for two days in Eurystheus's palace gardens. Then she jumped over the wall and ran back to the woods of Ceryneia, where she has lived happily ever since.

The journey was not going well. Atticus was sure they were lost. He stumbled over a boulder on the path and sat down heavily. He had terrible blisters.

"Up you get, Atticus," said Georgios, running over to help him up.

Georgios was Glaucus's nephew, a boy who helped the actors with their costumes. He was brilliant at designing masks, and Atticus often watched him in the evenings as he sewed and cut and bound together the costumes for the next day's performance.

"You're as strong as a bull!" grunted Atticus as Georgios hauled him to his feet. "But I'll bet you're not as strong as that Cretan bull Heracles had to capture. Just imagine! They say he caught it in the city near my village!"

The Fire Breather

King Minos of Crete had a problem. A gigantic bull was rampaging all over his island, rooting up the trees with his enormous horns, and trampling the crops with his huge feet.

"I need a hero to deal with this animal," he said to himself. "I wonder if my friend Eurystheus would lend me Heracles."

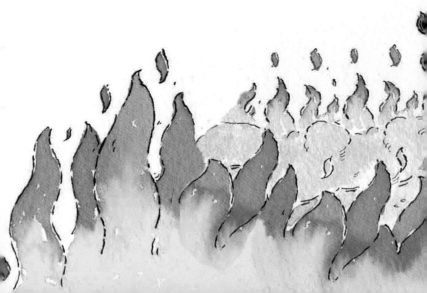

Eurystheus was delighted. He needed another task for Heracles, and this one sounded perfect.

"Bring the bull back here at once," he commanded. "I can use it against my enemies. It will be better than a whole army!"

When Heracles arrived in Minos's wonderful palace, the king was in the middle of a feast.

He was very pleased to see Heracles. "Sit down! Try some of these larks' wings – or perhaps a little simmered turtle egg."

Just then a messenger ran in. "Your Majesty!" he said, bowing and panting. "The citizens of Cydonia are terrified.

The bull has driven them all into one house, and he's stamping and snorting and breathing fire from his nostrils. They are trapped!"

Heracles leapt up. "No time for feasting, your Majesty," he said. "I'll be off!"

And he grabbed his weapons and followed the messenger out of the door.

The streets of Cydonia were deserted, but from the end of the city came a dreadful screaming and wailing, together with a loud thudding sound.

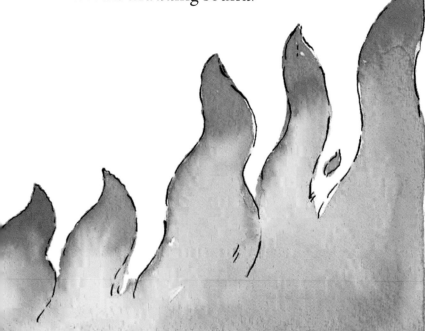

As Heracles ran up, the bull was charging at the door of a large house. His fiery breath had set all the grass alight, and men and women and children were hanging out of the windows, throwing water at it with buckets drawn from the well in the courtyard.

Heracles took a deep breath and bellowed. The bull turned round at once. His little eyes turned scarlet with rage, and sparks flew from his giant hooves.

Heracles held out his arms, and as the bull charged at him; he somersaulted on to its back.

The bull was very surprised indeed! It ran around the whole island of Crete, trying to throw Heracles off.

But Heracles held on with all his might, and squeezed the bull's ribs with his strong legs until it had no breath left, and collapsed on the ground exhausted.

Heracles threw a strong iron chain around its neck, and made it swim behind his boat all the way to the mainland. Then he dragged it back to Tiryns, right into the throne room.

When the bull could breathe again, it started to bellow.

"Take it to Hera's temple!" squeaked King Eurystheus, quickly hopping into the safety of his bronze jar again. "I give it to her as a gift."

But Hera didn't want the bull, so she sent it running all over Greece, until it was so tired that it lay down and died.

Heracles went and looked into the jar. "So, little cousin," he asked. "What would you like me to bring you next?"

There was a huge crowd in the amphitheatre at Sikyon all cheering and clapping loudly as the players bowed and bowed again. Atticus clapped too – he was very happy not to be lost in the woods any more.

Later, he and Glaucus went to an inn with the rest of the actors.

"Feasting is all very well," grumbled Glaucus as they stumbled home late that night, "but not when you have to be up and off early in the morning. Come on, Atticus. Cheer us up with a story."

"Those horse masks you used in the play," said Atticus. "They reminded me of another story about Heracles."

The Man-Eating Mares

Now that Heracles had succeeded in so many of the tasks he had been given by his cousin, King Eurystheus, he was feeling quite confident.

But the goddess Hera was furious. "You haven't given him anything difficult enough!" she screeched at the terrified king as he cowered in his bronze jar. "Heracles must fail, and then I shall have an excuse to punish him. All these successes are making his head even bigger than it was before!"

Eurystheus nodded. "I know, great Queen of Heaven," he said. "But he's just so good at everything."

 68

Then Hera leaned over and whispered in his ear. Eurystheus began laugh. "Perfect!" he sniggered, as he called for Heracles to attend him at once.

Hera had told Eurystheus to send Heracles to capture the four mares belonging to King Diomedes of Thrace.

Heracles didn't like horses very much – other animals were all right, but horses kicked and bit, and these mares were particularly nasty.

Whenever King Diomedes had strangers as guests, he would treat them to a feast, and if anyone had too much wine and got drunk he would chop them up and feed them to his horses. The mares had got used to eating human flesh, and every time a new groom came near them, they would crunch great lumps out of him with their sharp teeth.

Heracles sailed to Thrace, and when he landed, he tied up his boat and went boldly up to the king's palace.

When King Diomedes saw this fine-looking stranger, he smiled a wicked smile.

"A huge man like that will feed my horses for a week!" he thought, as he gave orders for a feast to be prepared, and invited Heracles to join him.

Diomedes poured cup after cup of wine
for Heracles, but Heracles secretly tipped
them behind the silk cushions without
anyone noticing. Soon he pretended to
go to sleep, and snored loudly.

When he felt King Diomedes start to
tie up his arms and legs, he leapt up.

"Wretched king!" he roared,
brandishing his club. "You shall suffer
the same fate you intended for me!"

And whacking the king on the head he

lifted him up, and threw him into the brass manger in the mares' stable. The four horses gobbled the king up right away, but as soon as they finished the last mouthful, they became calm and docile, and allowed Heracles to put on their golden bridles and lead them away to his boat.

"Your man-eating horses, dear cousin," he said as they trotted behind him into Eurystheus's throne room. The horses licked their lips and looked at Eurystheus hungrily.

"L—lock th—them in the s—s—tables," stuttered Eurystheus from the safety of his bronze jar.

And up on Olympus, Hera looked down and gnashed her teeth in rage as she saw that Heracles had succeeded once again in completing an impossible task.

Greek Beasts and Heroes and where to find them ...

Atticus tells stories of Heracles' final adventures in *The Harp of Death*, and you can read about the mighty hero in *The Flying Horse* too, which is next in the series.

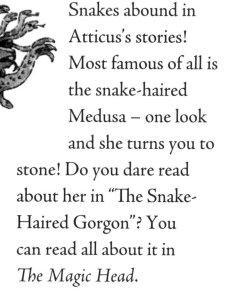

Snakes abound in Atticus's stories! Most famous of all is the snake-haired Medusa – one look and she turns you to stone! Do you dare read about her in "The Snake-Haired Gorgon"? You can read all about it in *The Magic Head*.

Wouldn't you like to find out how poor Pelops ended up in that stew – and how he survived? Read "The Terrible Feast" (it's in the book called *The Dolphin's Message*).

The ancient Greeks (and their gods) celebrated with fabulous feasts. (If only we had parties like that now!) But sometimes celebrations didn't go so well. Read about how a feast fit for a hero was spoilt by some most unwelcome guests in "The Ship of Heroes" which you'll find in *The Dragon's Teeth*.

Cowardly King Eurystheus hid inside a jar which was filled with oil. For a tale of another jar with much more dangerous contents, look for the first book in the series and read the title story, "The Beasts in the Jar".

For another tale of a bull who behaved in a surprising way, read "The Bull from the Sea" in *The Magic Head*.

Greek Beasts and Heroes
have you read them all?

1. *The Beasts in the Jar*
2. *The Magic Head*
3. *The Monster in the Maze*
4. *The Dolphin's Message*
5. *The Silver Chariot*
6. *The Fire Breather*
7. *The Flying Horse*
8. *The Harp of Death*

Available from August 2010:
9. *The Dragon's Teeth*
10. *The Hero's Spear*
11. *The One-Eyed Giant*
12. *The Sailor Snatchers*